Dr. Paul Witty, Director, Psycho-Educational Clinic, Northwestern University, says: "The Developmental Reading Program is best served with balanced reading which includes a wide variety of self-selection material in addition to the basic books."

MYSTERY OF THE FARMER'S THREE FIVES can be read by a child in the upper first grade. Over ninety per cent of the one hundred and forty-five word vocabulary is from *The First Thousand Words for Children's Reading.*

Mystery of
The Farmer's Three Fives

by Margaret Friskey

Illustrations by Lucy and John Hawkinson

CHILDRENS PRESS, CHICAGO

There once was a farmer
who had a few ducks.
A few are not many.

But a few are more than two.

"I have a few ducks,"
said the farmer.
"I have more than two."
"Now look here," said
the farmer's wife. "Just how
many ducks do you have?"

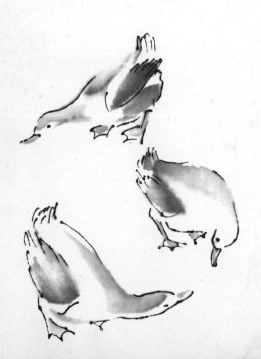

"I see
three in the corner
of the yard," said
the farmer.

"Oh, no," said his wife. "I see

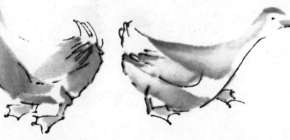

two in the
middle of the yard."

"I see five," said the
little boy.
"Hush!" said his mother.

"I see
four ducks

in the middle of the yard,"
said the farmer.

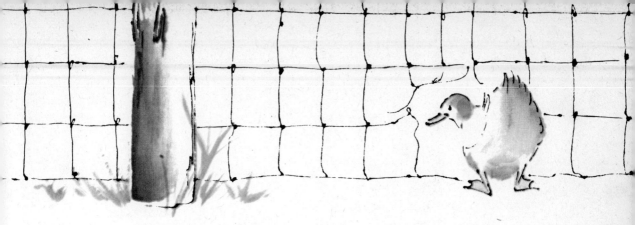

"I see one duck by the hole
in the fence," said his wife.
"One is almost none and that's
how many you have!"

"I see five," said the boy.
"Hush!" said the farmer.

The farmer and his wife
could not agree.

At last one day the farmer
said, "I see two ducks."

"And I see
two ducks," said his wife.

The boy said, "I see
four ducks.

One duck went away through
the hole in the fence."

"Hush!" said the farmer.
"Let me think. How many
ducks are a few for a farmer?"

"Look now and you can see,"
said the boy.

Five ducks in one long row
were walking away down the road.
All the ducks had gone away
through the hole in the fence.

"See," said the farmer. "FIVE!
Five are a fine few for a farmer."

"But five ducks that are gone
are no ducks," said his wife.
"You have none. Not any.
That's how many."
Then the wife said,
"All you have is
one hole in your fence."
"Ah, so," said the farmer.
"One small hole.
Ducks that are
as small as one small hole
can go through it."

"They are gone," said his wife.

"Go," said the farmer to the boy. "Go catch the ducks and trade them for a few pigs. Pigs are bigger than the hole in the fence. I will be the farmer who has a few pigs."

"More than two pigs?"
asked his wife.

"We shall see," said the
farmer.

The boy got four pigs for
the five ducks. They went

this way,

and that way,
as he drove them home.

"Four pigs are more than
two pigs," said the farmer.
"It is good to have a few
pigs," said his wife and she
was content.

But the pigs were not.

They pushed and poked at the
hole in the fence until it was
as big as a pig.

Then one after another the
pigs went away through the
hole in the fence.

"Catch the pigs," said the
farmer to the boy. "Trade them
for goats. Goats are bigger
than the hole in the fence.
Ah, it will be good to have a
few goats."

"More than two goats?" asked
his wife.

"We shall see," said the farmer.

The boy got three goats
for the four pigs.

"Ah," said the farmer, "three
goats are a fine few for a farmer."

But he did not have his goats
for long.

The goats butted at the hole
in the fence until it was as big
as a goat.

Away they went.

"You are a fine one!" cried
the wife. "Now all you have is
one BIG hole in your fence."

"Ah, so," said the farmer. "Now
I don't have a few of anything."

"Mend that big hole in your
fence," said his wife.

And the farmer did.

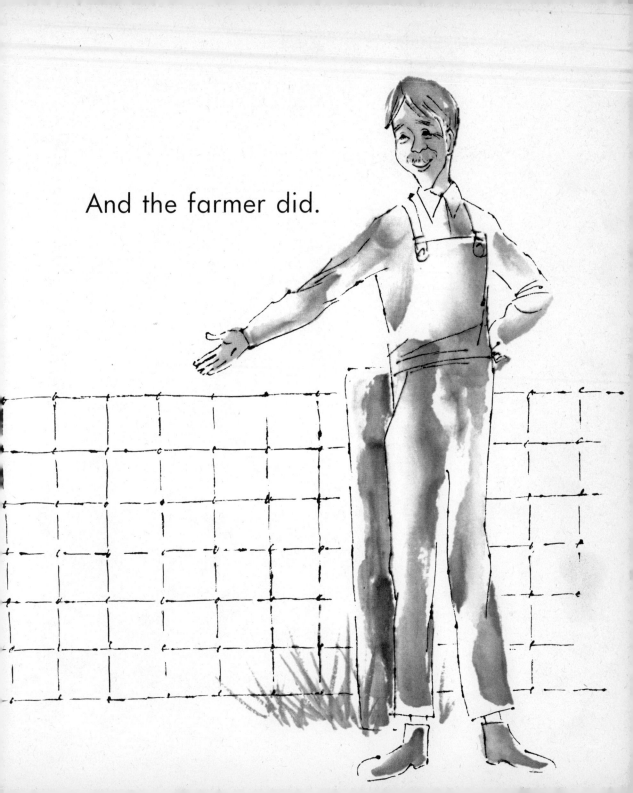

The boy went after the three goats

and traded them for two colts.

"Do we have a few colts?" asked
the wife.

"No. We have two colts," said
the farmer. "Just a couple of
colts. A pair."

"It is good to have two colts,"
said his wife.

The colts ran this way and that
way in the fenced-in yard. Then
one fine day, they jumped clear
over the fence and went away
down the road.

"You are a fine one!" said the
wife. "Now you don't even have
a hole in your fence."

"Alas! What shall we do?"
said the farmer.

The boy went after the colts
and traded them for

one fat, quiet cow.

"Now," said the farmer, "I am the farmer with one fat cow."

"It is good to have one cow," said his wife. And it was.

The cow stayed quietly in the fenced-in yard. And what a cow!

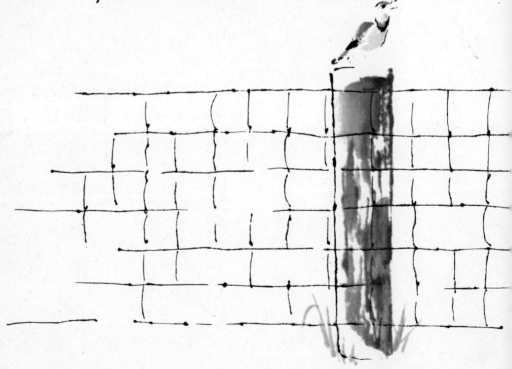

She gave milk
and cream.

The wife made butter
and cheese.

The boy traded butter and cheese
for the five ducks.

Then, later, the boy traded
butter and cheese for the
four pigs,

and then for the three goats,

and the two colts.

The wife looked at all the
animals in the fenced-in yard.

"My, what a fine few you do
have," she said to the farmer.

"There are more than a few,"
said the boy. "Now there are
many. I see three fives."

"How can that be?" asked
the farmer.

"The first five is all ducks,"
said the boy.

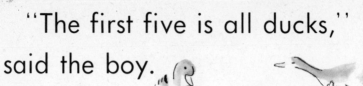

"The second five is three
goats and two colts.

"And the third five
is four pigs and one cow."

"Well now," said the farmer, "that is something to think about. But I will have to think about it later. Now I am the farmer who has a few chores. Three fives, hm!"

The boy went to help his father
with the chores.

When they had finished their work,
the farmer said, "Come into the
fenced-in yard with me."

"I will think about my three fives,"
said the farmer.

"Now I see five threes," said the
boy. "It comes to the same thing."

"Oh, hush!" said
the farmer. "Now
I must think
about
THAT."

WORDS I CAN READ IN THIS BOOK

*Skill-builders. Words that are beyond *The First Thousand Words for Children's Reading*

a
about
after
*agree
all
almost
and
animals
another
any
are
as
ask
at
away

be
bigger
boy
but
*butt
butter
by

can
catch
cheese
*chores
clear

*colts
come
*content
corner
could
*couple
cow

day
did
do
don't
down
drove

even

farmer
fat
fence
few
fine
finished
first
five
for
four

gave

go
*goats
gone
good
got

had
happy
he
help
here
his
hole
home
how
*hush

I
in

jump
just

knew

last
later
let
little

live
long
look

made
many
me
mend
middle
milk
more
mother
my

no
none
not
now

of
oh
on
once
only
over

pair
pigs
*poke

*push

quiet

ran
road
row

said
second
see
shall
she
small
so
something
stay

than
that
the
their
them
then
there
they
think
third
this

three
through
to
trade
two

until

walk
was
way
we
well
went
were
who
will
*wife
what

yard
you